This book
belongs to

Sleepy Snuggles

Words by
Diana Murray

Pictures by
Charles Santoso

CLARION BOOKS
An Imprint of HarperCollins Publishers

Snuggle-bunny, snuggle-bunny,
hop in bed, my dear.
I'll tuck you in the garden leaves
and kiss your floppy ear.

Snuggle-bear, snuggle-bear,
rest your furry paws.

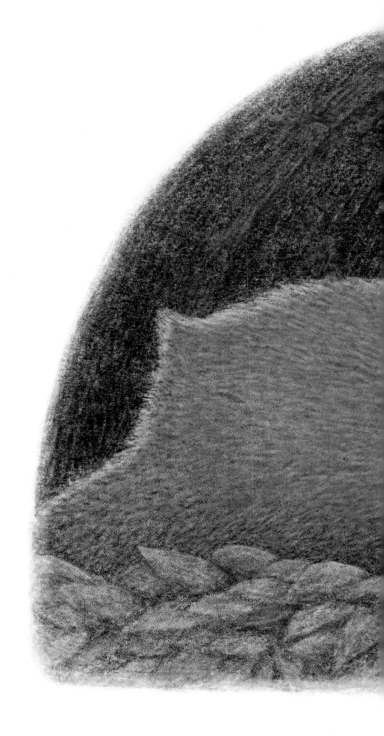

I'll tuck you in our cozy den
and kiss your tiny claws.

Snuggle-bee, snuggle-bee,
oh so honey-sweet,
I'll tuck you in our golden hive
and kiss your busy feet.

Snuggle-chick, snuggle-chick,
not another peep!

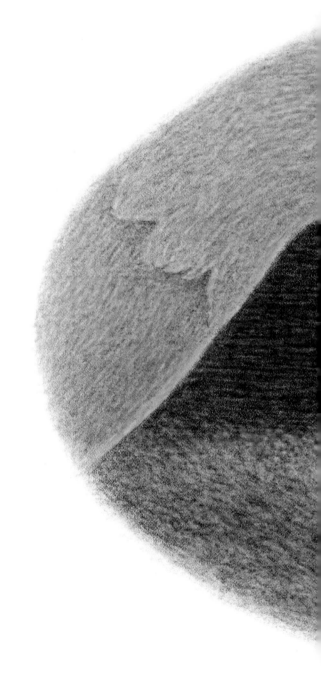

I'll tuck you in our feathered nest
and kiss your pointy beak.

Snuggle-lamb, snuggle-lamb,
leap right into bed.
I'll tuck you in a grassy field
and kiss your woolly head.

Snuggle-piglet, snuggle-piglet,
muddy through and through,
I'll tuck you in our comfy pen
and kiss your tummy too!

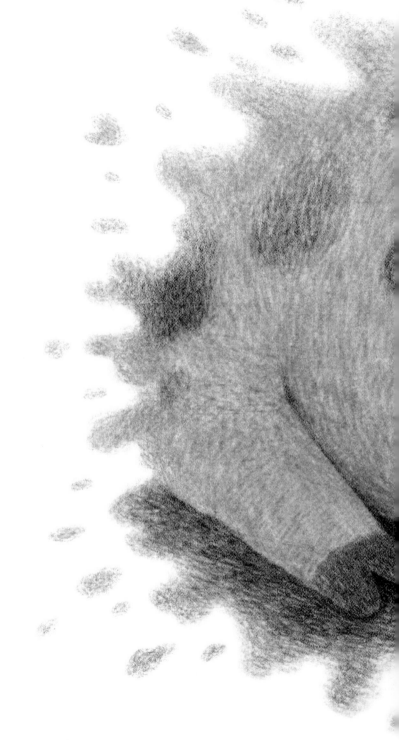

Snuggle-duckling, snuggle-duckling,
not another quack!

I'll tuck you in the swaying reeds
and kiss your downy back.

Snuggle-fish, snuggle-fish,
night is closing in.
I'll tuck you in the moonlit pond
and kiss your shiny fin.

Snuggle-frog, snuggle-frog,
under dreamy skies,

I'll tuck you in a lily pad
and kiss your sleepy eyes.

Snuggle-robin, snuggle-robin,
hear the crickets sing.
I'll tuck you in our willow tree
and kiss your weary wing.

Snuggle-baby, snuggle-baby,
stars are shining bright.
I'll tuck you in your blanket now . . .
with one last kiss good night.

For Kate and Jane, who make
Mama Duck proud —D.M.

For moms everywhere —C.S.

Clarion Books is an imprint of HarperCollins Publishers. • Sleepy Snuggles • Text copyright © 2024 by Diana Murray • Illustrations copyright © 2024 by Charles Santoso • All rights reserved. Manufactured in Italy. No part of this book may be used or reproduced in any manner whatsoever without written permission except in the case of brief quotations embodied in critical articles and reviews. For information address HarperCollins Children's Books, a division of HarperCollins Publishers, 195 Broadway, New York, NY 10007. • www.harpercollinschildrens.com • Library of Congress Control Number: 2023948454 • ISBN 978-0-06-325523-4 The artist used Photoshop, Procreate, and handmade textures to create the illustrations for this book. • Typography by Whitney Leader-Picone
24 25 26 27 28 RTLO 10 9 8 7 6 5 4 3 2 1 • First Edition